Sebi
and the Land of Cha Cha Cha

Roselyn Sánchez
and Eric Winter

illustrated by
Nivea Ortiz

celebra

It was El Carnaval Latino. The dancers in the street twirled and swirled, their feet moving like magic.

"Oh Mommy," said Sebi, watching from the sidewalk. "What is that dance? I want to do it!"

"It's the Cha Cha Cha," said her mother. "When you're a little older, you can take lessons."

"Let's try it," said Sebi to her friend Keeke.

"Do boys dance like that?" Keeke asked.

Sebi's grandmother nodded. "In Latin dancing, the boys lead the way."

"What about the girls?" asked Sebi.

Her mother smiled. "The girls glide with graceful strength."

As Sebi and Keeke took a few uncertain dance steps, a bright green bird fluttered into sight.

"Oh, look!" said Sebi's mother. "That's a *Cotorra*."

The *Cotorra* flapped its wing, as if it was waving at them, before it flew away.

"The *Cotorra* wants us to follow it," said Sebi. "I just know it."

Sebi and Keeke squeezed into the bushes. As they crawled in deeper, the smells around them got sweeter. They heard Latin music again. When they found their way to the other side, it was clear they weren't in the park anymore.

"*¡Hola!*" said the Cotorra. "Welcome to the Land of Cha Cha Cha."

"*¡Bienvenidos!*" said another beautiful bird. "I am the *Cha Cha Cha Cacatúa*. Would you like to learn my dance, the Cha Cha Cha?"

"Yes, yes, yes!" Sebi cried.

"First stand like this in dance position and repeat after us. One leg forward and step and step, step, step . . . One leg backward and step, step, step.

"Now, make circles with your hips—forward circle, backward circle!"

"*Cha cha cha, one and two and three!*"

"CHA CHA CHA!" Sebi shouted.

"Cha Cha Cha!" shouted Keeke.

"*¡Muy bien!*" said the **Cacatúa**. "Very good."

"*Well done!*" said some monkeys, swooping down from the trees.
"*¿Cómo están?* How are you? We are the **Merengue Monkeys**, and that is
what we dance. Would you like to learn the Merengue?"
"Yes, yes, yes!" Sebi shouted.
"*Claro,*" Keeke said. "Of course."

"Excellent," said the tallest *Merengue Monkey*. "Take these brooms and begin sweeping the ground.
"March while you swing your hips from side to side," he went on.

"Too stiff," said the littlest monkey. "You are not robots—you are dancers! Bend one knee at a time. The more you bend, the more your hips swing. *Now let's merengue!*"

"Now, Keeke, put down your broom and dance with Sebi," said the tallest *Merengue Monkey.* "Sebi, bend your elbow and hold up your hand. Keeke, take her hand and turn her."

"*¡WEPA!*" said the monkeys together. "*Well done!*"

"*BRAVO! BRAVO!*" said some squirrels, watching from the trees above them.

"Who are you?" asked Sebi.

"We are the *Samba Squirrels!*" said the biggest one. "Would you like to learn the Samba?"

"*¡Sí, sí, sí!*" shouted Sebi and Keeke.

The biggest squirrel nodded. "Let's start by all holding hands.
Then put your knees together and bounce to the beat.
"Bend your knees and bounce!" said the smallest squirrel.

"Now you're ready," said the smallest squirrel. "Just partner up and *Samba*."
"*¡Fantástico!*" said all the *Samba Squirrels*. "*Fantastic!*"

When they stopped to catch their breath, Sebi heard her mother calling.

"I'm afraid we must go," said Sebi. *"¡Adiós!* And *muchas gracias* for welcoming us to the Land of Cha Cha Cha."

The birds and animals nodded. *"Adiós*, Sebi. *Adiós*, Keeke. And remember—keep practicing!"

"There you are," said Sebi's mother. "*El Carnaval* is about to end!"

"Mommy, look!" Sebi said proudly. "Granny, watch what we can do."

Sebi and Keeke danced, and turned, and bounced to the beat of the distant carnival. "Oh, my!" said Sebi's mother. "You two look like you're ready to start Latin dancing now." Sebi and Keeke laughed.

"You know what, Mommy?" said Sebi. "We've already started!"

To our beautiful daughter Sebella Rose,
you make our hearts dance! And Mota . . . forever our angel.
—R.S. and E.W.

To my sweet Tai, faithful companion.
—N.O.

About the dances:

Cha Cha Cha: (also known as Cha Cha) is a style of music and dance from Cuba. It was created around the 1950s. The Cha Cha is energetic with a steady beat. The name is derived from the shuffling sound of the dancer's feet.

Merengue: is a style of Dominican music and dance. Partners hold each other in a closed position. The "merengue típico" originated in the rural northern valley region around the city of Santiago in Dominican Republic.

Samba: is a lively, rhythmical dance of Afro Brazilian origin that started in Rio de Janeiro in the early twentieth century. The basic movement involves a straight body and a bending of one knee at a time.

CELEBRA CHILDREN'S BOOKS
Penguin Young Readers Group
An imprint of Penguin Random House LLC
375 Hudson Street, New York, NY 10014

A Penguin Random House Company

Copyright © 2017 by Roselyn Sánches and Eric Winter

ISBN 9780399583636
Manufactured in China
1 3 5 7 9 10 8 6 4 2